Tapestry Press

*To Talin
With love,
Nancy Wilson Taylor*

PAISLEY PONY
AND
PLAID PUPPY MEET

Nancy Wilson Taylor

ISBN 978-1-64458-227-5 (paperback)
ISBN 978-1-64458-229-9 (hardcover)
ISBN 978-1-64458-228-2 (digital)

Christian Faith Publishing, Inc.
832 Park Avenue
Meadville, PA 16335
www.christianfaithpublishing.com

Printed in the United States of America

You made all delicate, inner parts of my body
and knit me together in my mother's womb.
Thank you for making me so wonderfully
complex! Your workmanship is
marvelous—how well I know it.
You watched me as I was being formed
in utter seclusion, as I was woven
together in the dark of the womb.
You saw me before I was born. Every day my
life was recorded in your book. Every moment
was laid out before a single day had passed.
—Psalm 139:13-16

This is my commandment, that you love
one another as I have loved you.
—John 15:12

Paisley is a happy, curious pony. He loves to try new things and especially loves to play outside. Exploring the woods is his favorite thing of all.

Paisley mostly has good days, but there is something missing from his life. He does not have a best friend.

There are a few other animals that he plays with, but not that very best friend that you can always count on.

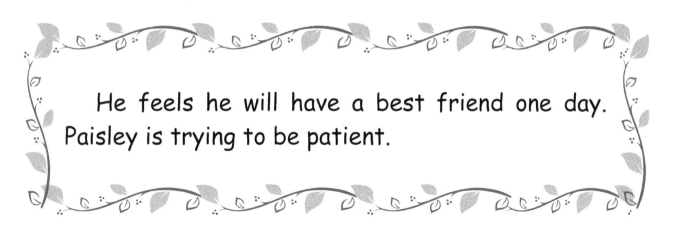

He feels he will have a best friend one day. Paisley is trying to be patient.

One beautiful sunny day, Paisley was on his way to a birthday party at Knit Kitten's house. He could not wait to see the other animals. He heard that Flannel Ferret, Denim Duck, and Gingham Guinea Pig would be there. Paisley thought that Madras Monkey would be there too, and he always tells the best jokes.

Knit lived on the other side of the woods in back of Paisley's house. Paisley walked that trail many times. On this day, about halfway to Knit's house, Paisley heard some cries coming from the left side of the trail behind some flowering bushes.

Paisley really wanted to keep walking and pretend he did not hear the crying. He could almost taste how delicious the cake was going to be.

Paisley knew the games would begin very soon.

Even though he really wanted to keep walking, Paisley had to stop and think for a moment. Should he keep walking and get to the party on time and enjoy the festivities?

Or should he stop and see if he could help whoever was crying behind those flowering bushes? He thought and thought...and then made the decision to help whoever was behind those bushes.

Paisley went over and peeked behind the bushes and saw a puppy with a cut on his paw. The puppy was very tired and was having a tough time making it back home by himself.

Paisley said, "Do you need some help?"

Plaid Puppy looked up and said, "Yes, thank you so much. I really hurt my paw over on that tree branch, and I can't make it home by myself."

Paisley offered his hoof to help him up and slowly they made their way to Plaid's house.

Paisley decided not to tell Plaid about how he gave up going to an awesome birthday party to stop and help him. He thought that might make Plaid feel bad for taking up his time. He made the right decision not telling him because along the way they shared many great stories about one another. They discovered they had so many great things in common.

Plaid forgot how much his paw hurt, and Paisley forgot about how he gave up going to a party to help someone in need.

Paisley did not know it at the time, but that decision to stop and help Plaid changed his life forever. Paisley and Plaid became very best friends.

And little did they know that in a cottage not too far away, the Tailor who made them was smiling.

About the Author

Nancy Wilson Taylor has a passion for children and young adults, knowing their worth in our Creator's eyes. She has been involved in children and youth programs for over twenty-one years. Nancy has been on numerous mission trips from Appalachia to Rwanda. She wants every child to know they were created with a plan and a purpose. Each person is valuable and vitally important.

Nancy lives just outside of Boston, Massachusetts. She resides with her husband of twenty-one years, John, and their five children—Shaw, Ashley, Ethan, Max, and Stephanny—who are all attending college. She loves attempting to organize the chaos of five kids, four rescue dogs, and four cats. To rejuvenate and restore, she loves to spend time with her family in Cape Cod, Massachusetts; York Beach, Maine; and St Augustine, Florida.

CPSIA information can be obtained
at www.ICGtesting.com
Printed in the USA
LVHW070031200819
628264LV00006B/96/P